Fat Boy

Janice Greene
AR B.L.: 3.1
Points: 1.0

UG

# FAT BOY

**Janice Greene**

**SERIES 3**

The Bad Luck Play

Breaking Point

Death Grip

**Fat Boy**

No Exit

No Place Like Home

The Plot

Something Dreadful Down Below

Sounds of Terror

The Woman Who Loved a Ghost

Development and Production: Laurel Associates, Inc.
Cover Illustrator: Black Eagle Productions

**SADDLEBACK** PUBLISHING · INC.
Three Watson
Irvine, CA 92618-2767

E-Mail: info@sdlback.com
Website: www.sdlback.com

ISBN 1-56254-428-4

Printed in the United States of America
07 06 05 04 03 02     9 8 7 6 5 4 3 2 1

I start walking toward the bus stop, tagging along behind some other kids, trying to blend in. They're laughing and talking—nobody notices me. If I'm lucky I'll stay invisible.

Then I hear footsteps behind me. "Sánte! *Sánnn-te!*" The voice calling my name is sing-song, taunting. It's Rubio! My stomach twists with an awful combination of fear and helpless anger.

More footsteps. "*Sánte! Sánte!*" Now I can hear that Rubio's whole gang is with him. I know I'm doomed.

I start running as fast as I can, which isn't very fast. I head toward the woods next to school. In 10 seconds, they've got me, Rubio grabbing one arm and Quinto the other. I squirm and thrash around, trying to get loose. But I know it's hopeless. There are just too many of them.

They push me to the ground. Dirt smears my face and goes up my nose. "Get his shoe off!" someone yells.

I go crazy, kicking and punching wildly, desperately. "No!" I yell. *"Don't!"*

Their hands are all over me, rough and hard. But their punches don't hurt much. What really hurts is my soul.

Then all seven of them grab me and I can't move. I feel my shoe being pulled off. I squeeze my eyes shut.

"Freak show!" hollers Rubio.

"Grrrross!" Quinto yells.

From all sides, their voices hit me like bombs. *"Yuck!" "Disgust-o!"*

One boy makes retching noises. Another screams in mock terror. "Auuugh! It's gonna get me! The curse of the clubfoot!"

Then one boy yells, "Bus!" and they all run off, laughing and yelling.

I sit up, wiping the dirt off my face with my shirt. And since no one can see me, I cry for a minute.

The next day, I'd do anything to stay home from school, but Mom insists. "You have to get an education," she always says. I don't tell her what I'm really learning, which is to hate.

We're in the middle of math class when the principal, Mr. McNulty, comes in. He brings in a new boy. The kid is kind of tall, but he's fat, too. A new victim for Rubio and his gang.

"This is Tino Morales," says Mr. McNulty. "I want all of you to please make Tino feel welcome here."

Somebody makes a fart sound, which Mr. McNulty ignores.

Tino looks around the room at everyone, checking them out. It doesn't seem to bother him that all the kids are staring at him. He's staring right back at them. In fact, he looks bored.

At lunch, I see Tino again. Now he's carrying a lunch bag and heading for the stairs.

Usually, I don't talk to anybody unless I have to. But today I surprise myself. "Wait!" I say, hurrying after him. "Don't go on the stairs."

He looks at me for a few seconds, one eyebrow raised high.

"This guy, Rubio, and his gang—that's their territory," I explain.

"They don't let anybody else use the stairs?" Tino asks.

"Sometimes if you're cool with them, it's okay—" I say.

"You think it's possible I could *ever* be cool with those guys?" he says. That eyebrow comes up again.

Suddenly, I feel like I could tell this guy anything. "Not in a million years," I say with a grin.

He laughs, and keeps on walking toward the stairs. Following him, I wonder if he's brave or crazy. Quinto and another guy, Bobby, see where Tino is headed. Of course they go right after him. I peek over the stairs just as Quinto and Bobby catch up to Tino.

"Hey, Fat Boy," Quinto snarls like the rat he is. "What are you doing here?"

"Going down the stairs, one step at a time," says Tino. "Is that a problem?"

Bobby says, "Yeah, the stairs are *our* territory—the Blades!"

"So I'm supposed to bow down and promise to never use the stairs again, is that it?" Tino says. His voice is sarcastic. He looks them up and down, and I know they're getting steamed.

Bobby turns to Quinto. "Guess the fat boy needs to be taught a lesson," he says. "Right?"

Quinto never gets a chance to answer. Tino lunges forward, slamming his big foot down on Quinto's instep. At the same time, he rams his fist into Bobby's stomach. Quinto yelps with pain

7

and Bobby doubles up, groaning. He looks like he's going to puke. I hurry away before someone sees me.

I'm walking to my last class when Tino catches up to me.

"Hey," he says. "Thanks for the warning."

"Uh—that's okay," I say lamely. I'm not used to talking to people.

"I needed to look out for those guys," Tino says.

"They'll get back at you," I say.

"Yeah, I can imagine," he says.

"Aren't you scared?" I say.

"I've been beat up a lot," he says with a shrug. "Hey, which bus do you take to get home?"

"The 31," I say.

"Me, too," he says. "I'll meet you at the bus stop after school."

"Okay," I say.

"I know where your locker is," he says. "See you later."

I watch him walk off and I notice

something amazing—Tino walks proud. Fat kids at Carmichael High don't usually walk like that. I wonder how long he'll last here.

**A**fter school, I get my books out of my locker. I wonder if he's going to show up. But Tino is one surprise after another. He comes around the corner.

We walk to the bus, and it's okay today: None of the Blades are around. "What's wrong with your right foot?" Tino asks.

I stare at him. I swear, nobody's asked me that since I was eight years old. They usually ask *someone else* what's wrong with me.

"It's a clubfoot," I say. "My foot's twisted. It's been that way ever since I was born."

"Huh. Anything you can do about it?" Tino says.

"If they'd done something right away,

they could have fixed it, but I think it's too late now," I say.

"It's all your fault," Tino says. "You should've been born rich. Then they would have taken care of it right away."

I grin. Another surprise. It actually feels *good* to talk about my foot.

"It's my fault, too—that I'm fat," he says. "I eat too much."

I start laughing. "Did you ever go on a diet?" I ask.

"Only about 17 times," he says. Now we're both laughing.

Tino gets off the bus and waves. I get off at the next stop and head to the day care center. I have to pick up my baby sister, Yoli.

When she sees my face she lights up like a candle. She comes running for a hug, calling "Sánte! Sánte!"

Everybody loves Yoli 'cause she's sweet and really pretty. People think I'm good-looking, too—until they see me walk. When Yoli's 16, like I am now, she won't want to be seen on the street with me. But right now, it's cool. I'm the sun, the moon, and the stars to her.

We walk home and watch TV for a while. Then I fix something to eat and Mom comes home. As usual, she looks exhausted. She works in a factory, making men's wallets. Her hands hurt all the time. That's because she does the same movements over and over. Sometimes I hear her crying when she's trying to fold laundry. Or maybe she's crying about something else.

After everyone goes to bed, I sit down at my drums. But I just play on the practice pad so I won't wake anybody up. My drums are the coolest thing I ever had. My uncle left them for me when he died three years ago. Even when there's no school, playing drums is the best part of the day—always.

When I see Tino at lunch the next day, he's got Runt with him. They look odd together. That's because Tino's tall and Runt's about as big as your average fifth-grader. After me, he's Rubio's favorite victim.

"Hey, man, we're starting a club," Tino announces. *The Outcasts.*

"Sounds good," I say. Everything Tino says sounds good to me.

"Runt says Loretta might join," Tino goes on. "We oughtta have a girl, right?"

"I don't know," I say. "She kind of keeps to herself."

"Keeps to herself?" Tino's eyebrow shoots up. "You mean, no one talks to her? No one sits with her at lunch?"

Runt starts laughing.

"No," I say. "I mean sometimes she gets mad and lashes out at people. She seems angry all the time."

"How about you?" says Tino. Suddenly he's serious, looking at me real close. "You look pretty quiet. Are you angry too? Would you like to feel Rubio's face under your foot?"

"Yeah," I say. Just the *idea* of doing that sounds so sweet!

"Let's go find Loretta," says Tino.

Loretta's sitting at the farthest corner of the schoolyard, where no one goes. When she sees us coming, she gathers up her stuff. She wants to be ready to leave if she decides to.

Loretta's not ugly, really. It's just that her neck looks too long and her head looks too small. Her nose is sort of hooked. Parts of her are pretty—but nobody seems to notice those.

"Hi," Tino says.

Loretta doesn't answer. She's tight, wary. I know the look because it's my look, too. She's waiting for the insult or the joke we're gonna pull on her.

"We're thinking of starting a club— the Outcasts," says Tino. His voice is respectful. "Would you like to join up?"

Loretta looks the three of us up and down. Then she smiles, just a little. "What's this club all about?" she asks.

"Fame and revenge," says Tino. "We're gonna meet somewhere tonight and talk about it. You want to come?"

We meet at my house. Yoli's so excited to have three big kids around she can hardly stand it. At bedtime, she kisses each of—uh—my friends. She cries when she has to leave the room. Then Mom comes home and the four of us go outside so we can talk in private.

Tino plunks down in the weeds behind the house. "So what do we want," he says, "besides Rubio's head on top of a stick?"

"I know. Why don't we enter the talent show," Loretta suggests shyly.

*The talent show.* The idea's so mind-boggling no one speaks for a minute.

"That's crazy," says Runt. "The talent

14

show is for the popular kids. It's—"

Tino interrupts. "Huh? You're saying there's no outcasts allowed? Let's *do* it!"

Somehow, with Tino here, anything seems possible. Runt gulps and says, "What would we do?"

"I play guitar," says Loretta.

"I play drums," I say.

"That's cool," says Tino. "Let's write a song. Something real, you know— something with an edge to it."

Loretta giggles. "Yeah, something that'll bite 'em in the butt," she says.

"Yeah!" I say.

"Hey, what about getting back at the Blades?" Runt says.

"Later," says Tino. His eyes are twinkling. "First we make our mark."

By 10:00 P.M., we've already got the first verse down.

After everyone leaves, I'm still fired up. Since I can't sleep, I write down ideas for song lyrics late into the night.

The next day, I actually feel like getting up. I'm excited, but nervous, too, all the way to school. I'm thinking about the Blades getting back at Tino. Then, in the hallway, I overhear some good news—Rubio's been suspended for a week. He got caught starting a fire in the boys' locker room. Tino's safe from the Blades for a while. Good! Without its head, the snake won't strike.

We all eat lunch at Loretta's corner. There's a big debate over the song. Everyone's been working on it, and everyone has different ideas. But even though the song isn't finished, Tino wants to see how we sound.

The next morning, Saturday, we meet in Tino's garage. Loretta surprises me. I thought she'd bring an acoustic guitar. But instead she shows up with her dad's old Fender. It sounds pretty

16

good, and the girl can actually *play*.

Loretta and I fool around with a few tunes. I've never played with anyone before, so at first we sound pretty awful.

"Let's work on the song," says Tino. We end up voting on our favorite lines. I'm happy when a lot of mine make the cut. Tino assigns me to work out the rest of the song. Then Loretta and I play again. Now we sound a little better.

Before we know it, it's late in the day. I need to go home to help Mom. All the way home, I'm smiling. When Yoli opens the door for me, I grab her and twirl her around the kitchen.

We work on our act every chance we get. We spend hours at my house or in Tino's garage, and I learn a lot about everybody. All I knew about Loretta was that she was angry. But now I find out she's funny, too. Runt likes a lot of my favorite bands. Tino was suspended for fighting three times at his old school.

Those guys learn a lot about me, too.

That's because I can't stop talking. It's the same with everybody—except Tino. The rest of us can't stop. It's like we've never said anything for years.

After five days, our song is coming together. We're feeling pretty good when Loretta says, "What about the tryouts?"

"You have to *try out* for the show?" says Tino.

"Yeah," she says. "In front of a bunch of teachers. They're gonna hear this and say, 'uh, sorry.' It's too—uh—too *angry*. They usually like upbeat stuff."

Tino turns to me, "That right, Sánte?" he asks.

I frown. "They won't like that line in the song about the Blades. Maybe we should take it out," I say.

"No, man. The song's good. I'll think of something," says Tino.

**T**he day of the talent show, Tino leads the four of us into the principal's office. Tino's T-shirt is tucked in and his hair is neatly combed. He smiles respectfully as he walks up to Principal McNulty's desk.

"Unfortunately, sir," Tino says, "we missed the talent show tryouts. The problem was that our guitar player was sick. But we do have an act that's fully rehearsed and ready to perform. And I can guarantee it's in good taste."

How could Mr. McNulty refuse such a polite young gentleman? He says, "That's fine, Tino. Tell Ms. Muñoz I said you can be added to the program."

Backstage, we watch the popular kids racing around. The girls' voices are shrill with excitement. The guys are joking loudly. We get a few curious stares, but mostly we're invisible—just like always.

When we get onstage, there's some snickering and a few hoots. Then Loretta does the intro, I come in, and Runt and Tino step up to the mike. Loretta and

I wait until everybody quiets down.
We want the audience to hear every
single word:

> You go to bed, good looking and
>     popular.
> But something in the night
>     grabs you by the jugular.
> Caught in a nightmare, you toss
>     to and fro.
> When you wake up, nothing's
>     like it was before.
> You're an outcast!
>
> Your good looks have vanished
>     without a trace.
> Nobody wants to see your ugly
>     face.
> Or maybe you're short and easy
>     to take down,
> Nobody cares if they pound you
>     to the ground.

*Or maybe you're fat and
   nothing fits right,
You're one huge joke from
   morning to night,
Or suppose you've got a clubfoot
   and you can't really run—
The Blades are gonna jump you
   just to have some fun.*

*You're an outcast! And try as
   you might,
You're society's reject! Just stay
   out of sight!
Stay out of sight! Stay out of
   sight!*

**W**hen we finish, there's a silence so dead it feels like the auditorium is empty. Then there's a little bit of applause here and there. We nod and walk off. But Tino, Loretta, Runt, and I feel like we've flown over the ocean.

Afterward, a few kids come up and say they liked it. Most kids just give us weird looks. Later, in my backyard, we celebrate by eating four packages of cookies Loretta brought over. Then Tino says, "Now, we move on to phase two. We *strike*."

Loretta frowns. "What do you mean, 'strike'?"

"You know—we get even," says Tino. "Anyone else tired of watching their back every second?"

"*Real* tired," Runt says bitterly.

"But how?" I say. "There's way too many of them."

Tino smiles slowly. "We take them one by one," he says.

Loretta looks doubtful. "I don't know," she says. But no one listens to her.

The next time we meet in Tino's garage. We practice fighting moves. Tino knows a lot. After an hour, I feel like a punching bag. But I'm learning how to get in a few blows of my own. Loretta isn't there. Nobody says anything about it. But I figure Tino just didn't tell her about the meeting.

We decide to bite the snake in the head. Rubio, who's coming back to school tomorrow, is our first target. I know that Rubio likes this girl, Chia. So I write a note that I hope will fool him. Here's what it says:

> *R: I've been thinking about you*
> *a lot since you were gone. Meet*
> *me at the wall tomorrow—C.*

I get to school real early and stick the note in his locker. The next time I see him, he's combing his hair. He has that look of anticipation. I feel a hot bubble of excitement and hate growing in my chest.

When the final bell rings, the Outcasts are the first kids out of the classrooms. We go separate ways to the woods, being careful that no one sees us. We meet at the crumbling brick wall that used to be part of someone's yard.

Tino passes out black ski masks he got at the discount store. When we put them on, my hands are shaking.

We crouch down behind the wall, which is about five feet high, and listen. We don't have long to wait. Soon we hear the crunch of leaves. Tino eases up behind a bush and peers over the wall. It's Rubio, and he's alone!

Then we get lucky. Rubio does something absolutely perfect. Turning away from us, he heaves up onto the wall and sits. In one second, Tino grabs his belt and yanks him over backward. He's on the dirt, and we're on him—kicking, punching, yelling.

I've got fire inside from years of hurt and rage. Every dirty thing I've been called, every stupid joke played on me, every nasty look comes boiling out through my fists and feet.

Rubio's lying there gasping, helpless, and Tino is on his chest. Rubio's forehead is bleeding. I see the fear in his eyes, and I feel a rush of power and cold cruelty. I bring my clubfoot down on his nose like a hammer. He screams and screams.

When I look at his bloody face, a wave of nausea comes over me. Then Tino pulls me away, and we run through the woods to a place by the lake. When we stop, I puke. I don't know why.

Later, when I get home, all I can see is his bloody face. Even when I play the drums, I see his face.

The next day Tino picks out a new spot to eat lunch. It's like he's trying to avoid Loretta now, but she finds us anyway.

"I hear that Rubio's nose is broken," she says accusingly.

"That's the best news I've heard all day," says Tino.

"You guys beat him up! And you know what that makes you?" she screams at us. "It makes you as bad as they are!"

Tino looks her up and down, one black eyebrow raised. "I thought girls were supposed to be tough. Guess not," he says with a sneer.

"That's right, Tino. Go ahead. Put me down 'cause I won't stoop to your level," says Loretta. Her cheeks are bright pink with anger.

"See you later, Loretta. Like *never*," says Tino. "I was getting tired of looking at your ugly face anyway."

Loretta leaves without a word, and I know she's hurting. Suddenly, I really want to talk to her.

I start after her. "Loretta, wait!" I call out. But then Tino puts his hand on my shoulder. "Let her go," he says.

I shrug off his hand.

"*I said let her go!*" Tino shouts. His voice is hard as stone.

Two weeks ago, I would have slunk back to my seat. But now things are

26

different. *I'm* different. I keep going toward Loretta.

"Keep going and that's it, man," Tino says. "Don't come back."

"I'm supposed to *obey* you?" I say. "Like you're the dictator or something?"

"Shut up!" he yells, coming after me. His face is twisted in a sneer. Now *he's* the one who's ugly, not Loretta.

"What are you gonna do, fight me?" I say. "Go ahead, you'll probably beat me."

He gives me a hard shove. "Okay, then go after her, *wuss!*" he says. He turns away and walks back to Runt. I don't see Loretta until after school.

"Loretta? Could I just tell you what happened?" I ask her.

She nods and I tell her everything. I even tell her how I got sick afterward.

"It was what you did that made you sick to your stomach, Sánte," she says.

I nod. "I wanted to get even with Rubio for years," I say. "Now I get my revenge and it just feels like nothing."

27

"Rubio's gonna beat you, first chance he gets," says Loretta.

She's right. And I'm pretty sure Tino won't be around to defend me. I stay awake all night, thinking about it. The next morning, I walk up to Rubio in the hallway. He's surrounded by the Blades, as usual. But I just walk right through them. Rubio stares at me, angry and amazed. He can't believe I've got the nerve to face him.

Rubio has a thick, white bandage on his nose. His face is swollen and puffy. But he'll have his good looks back in a couple of weeks. Even hurt, he seems confident. But now I know something I didn't know before. Some invisible part of him is weak and crippled, or he wouldn't have to beat up people.

Before Rubio can say anything, I say, "Meet me after school at the wall. If you want to fight me, okay. But this time it's gotta be one on one—just you and me."

I turn and walk away before he can

answer. Then I tell Loretta what I did. She understands. Especially when I say I'm tired of scuttling around like a frightened rat, waiting for the cat to pounce. Loretta is a cool girl.

It's a weird day. A girl in my math class, Mari, actually comes up and talks to me. She says she liked my playing in the talent show. Then she tells me she plays the keyboard. I can't believe I'm so calm around her.

After lunch, Runt finds me. "You *challenged* Rubio? Serious?" he asks.

"Yeah," I say.

"You are so crazy, man," he says.

"Is Tino still mad at me?" I ask.

"He's not mad. He just hates your guts," says Runt, walking away.

I feel a pang of loneliness, wishing I had Tino to urge me on.

My last class ends. I walk through the woods in a daze. Kids are walking on both sides of me, keeping their distance. I know they're coming to watch the slaughter.

When I reach the wall, about 20 kids are standing around. Loretta's there and Chia's there, and all the Blades. Rubio's pacing around, looking like he can't wait to deck me. A cold lump of fear settles in my stomach. I force myself to speak. "After this, Rubio, you gotta leave me alone. Just let me be."

Rubio just swears. "You broke my nose! I'm gonna kill you!" he yells. He lunges at me. I manage to jump back. I'm hoping he's so mad he'll fight stupid.

I figure he's gonna go for my face. He does. He swings, and I swerve, getting in a blow to his throat. He coughs and gags, so I get in another hit at his ribs. When he grunts, I know it hurt.

I get in another blow to his chest. Then I see Tino standing off to the side. I try to read his expression, and that makes me a second too slow. Rubio punches me—hard—right above the ear.

My head is ringing. Before I can land another blow, Rubio socks me on one side of my nose. I feel like my brain has been shaken loose from my skull! Then I'm on the ground. "This is it," I'm thinking. "He's really gonna kill me."

Rubio is bending over me, his angry face close to mine. Then suddenly, I can see Loretta's face, and Chia's, and some other kids, too.

"Stop it! That's enough!" they're yelling. They pull Rubio away. He's yelling and swearing, but he doesn't come after me again. Someone pulls me up in a sitting position. My nose must be bleeding, because there's blood all over my shirt.

"Sánte! Are you okay?" It's Mari.

I can't answer. I look at the worried faces around me and I'm amazed. But I can't help wondering where Tino is. Why doesn't he help me?

**A** week has gone by since the fight with Rubio. My face looks awful, but nothing's broken. Mom was really upset, but I keep telling her I'm okay. And for once I'm not lying. Mari says that Rubio's gonna leave me alone now. She says that his rep would suffer if he didn't. Imagine that—*somebody's rep would suffer if they picked on me.*

I've been eating lunch with Mari and Loretta every day. They're coming over tomorrow, along with Mari's brother.

I still miss Tino all the time. When he and Runt pass me in the hall, they look right through me. Maybe he'll never forgive me for going against him. But I keep thinking that if it hadn't been for him, I wouldn't have friends now. I wouldn't be walking around school with my head up high. I *owe* him—you know? Someday, maybe tomorrow, I'm going to tell him that.

8583